The Amish Caregiver

Hannah Schrock

Prologue

"Mamm, you must try to drink some more broth."

Eve sighed as her mother turned her head from the spoon offered her. She was eating less and less every day. Eve prayed, as she had so many times a day, that Gott would spare her. The prayer was a constant one. Almost like breathing. In and out. Spare my mother. In and out. Spare my mother.

For years, Eve had been caring for everyone and everything around her. Her parents would smile lovingly whenever she brought home a bird with a broken wing, or insisted a stray cat stay with them. Sometimes it would become too much even for them, loving people though they were. "This house has become a zoo," her Mamm would say with a furrowed brow. But as soon as she saw the look of pure hope on her daughter's face, Ruth Lantz would smile. She had known how rare it was for a person to be so totally dedicated to the welfare of others.

"Gott has a special plan for all of our lives," Ruth would say, pulling Eve toward her for an affectionate hug. “I believe He wishes for you to help others when they are most in need.”

Eve had taken that to heart. Whenever a member of their community became ill, she was the first at the door to offer her services. Even if it was something as simple as helping with chores so the family didn’t fall behind, or preparing food to take to the sick person. She had helped nurse little Noah Yoder back to health when he had a grievous cough and fever.

Perhaps if she had been born into the world of the Englisch, she would have studied to be a doctor. She thought about that sometimes, what it would be like to learn all the mysteries of the body and how to heal a person’s every illness. How exciting that might be. But only Gott should know such things. He knew best. It was merely up to people to do His work. Too much knowledge, and a person might begin to think they knew better than Gott.

Still, as she sat at her dying mother’s bedside, Eve wished there were more she could do.

Mamm was holding up well, though. She was bearing her illness with the same strength and faith which had carried her throughout life. She was never without a kind word on her lips or a prayer in her heart. Oftentimes, she and Eve would pray together.

Eve wiped her mother's brow. She had fallen asleep, her chest rising and falling in shallow breaths. It was only a matter of time.

She took the opportunity to fetch a fresh basin of water and clean towels. Downstairs, her Daed was sitting by the hearth. It was unusual for him to be indoors in the early afternoon—normally, he would have been outside with his son, Caleb, and the farm hands.

"Daed?" Eve placed a gentle hand on her father's shoulder. He seemed to have aged years in only the few short weeks since receiving the news of his wife's cancer. "Can I do anything for you?"

He did not look up at her, but gently patted her hand. "No, thank you, dochder. You are doing so much already. It is a comfort to me that you care so well for your mother in these final days." So he had accepted the fact of his wife's impeding death. For days, he hadn't. He had prayed more fervently than all the rest, sure that Gott would hear him and cure his beloved wife.

"Perhaps you should go and speak with her," Eve said. "She is sleeping at the moment, but she never sleeps for very long. The pain is too great. Every time she moves it wakes her."

He let out a shuddering sigh, and Eve wondered if she had misspoken. For some reason, though she had always thought of her father as the strongest man in the world, it appeared as though she was even stronger than him. It was a strange feeling.

"I will see her shortly. I must go out and help Caleb with the plowing." He sighed. He patted Eve's shoulder. "You are a blessing to us."

Eve didn't see it that way at all. She was merely doing what she felt compelled to do. Her parents had worked hard for years to ensure that Eve and her younger brother lived a good life and had their needs met. The least Eve could do was to care for her mother.

Neighbors visited throughout the day, checking on Ruth and asked how Eve was getting along in her caregiving. "You must take time to rest," Mrs. Lapp said, holding a hand to Eve's forehead as though to check for temperature. Eve only smiled and assured her family's closest neighbor that she was doing well and getting all the rest she needed. Inside, she reminded herself that she didn't need as much rest as an older person might. She was young, only eighteen, and strong. She had the fortitude to spend the long, sleepless nights by her mother's bedside in case she needed anything. Ruth had been moved to Eve's bedroom, so she might be more comfortable and not disturb her husband, who needed to be up before the sun to attend to the needs of the farm.

After a while, it was just Eve and Ruth again. The others were kind to visit, but they had their own families and homes to attend to. The evening meal would have to be prepared.

"Eve." It was a thin whisper, one which Eve had to lean close to hear.

"Yes, Mamm?"

"I am glad you are my dochder. You have a gift for caring. Use that to help others, but take care of yourself, too. Do not wear yourself down. And always put Gott first."

Eve nodded, tears filling her eyes. Her mother's breathing had become more labored. Just the act of speaking so few words had exhausted her.

She took the chance, running downstairs and out the door to call for her father and brother. The time had come—somewhere inside, she knew it.

By the time they reached Ruth's bedside, it was too late.

The Storm

Two Years Later

Eve jumped at the sound of thunder. She peered out the window over the sink, where she washed the supper dishes. Rain fell so hard and fast; it was impossible to see anything but sheets of water.

The storm was bound to be a terrible one. All day, dark, angry clouds had raced across the sky. The air had fairly crackled with electricity, somehow feeling heavier. Anyone accustomed to summer storms knew there was a strong one brewing.

The thunder boomed again, this time accompanied by a zigzagging bolt of lightning. Eve's heart raced, though she knew she was far too old to be afraid of a silly storm. She would have felt better had her father and brother been inside the house with her, but the odds were they were in the barn, tending to the horses. The animals became so easily spooked at times like that.

She dried her hands on a towel, then took the chance to stepping outside to the covered porch. Rain pounded on the roof over her head, sounding like thousands of thudding hooves. A stampede. It was almost enough to make her cover her ears. She narrowed her blue eyes, hoping to catch a glimpse of her father or Caleb in the downpour. She could see nothing in the heavy rain.

She looked down at the ground beyond the porch. Water was already rising. This is terrible, she thought. Her garden might be drowned, to say nothing of the crops. She hoped it was a strong but fast-moving storm.

A sound floated to her ears just above the cacophony of thudding rain. Even looked back out toward the barn. There was someone there, waving his arms. Daed. He needed her help.

Thinking nothing of herself, Eve took off at a run. Instantly, she was soaked to the skin thanks to the downpour. She shielded her eyes from the driving rain, praying nobody was hurt.

"What is it?" she yelled, hoping to be heard over the storm.

"The horses! We weren't finished bringing them in before it started!" Sure enough, four of them were running loose in the paddock, terrified by the crashing thunder. “We have to get them into the barn!”

Eve nodded, turning to the paddock fence. It was dangerous to approach a spooked horse, but she had built quite a rapport with their horses over the years. She had a gentle nature which they responded to. Reminding herself to be calm, she shimmied through a small opening in the gate.

“Come, Lady,” she said, holding one hand to her favorite mare. “Come.”

The horse sniffed her hand, and she patted its head. Taking the reins, she led her to the barn, where Caleb was waiting.

They took turns, she and Caleb, calming then leading the horses inside. Rain ran down her face and beat down her back. Her shoes sank into the mud, making it more difficult to even lift her feet from the ground. It was hard work to say the least. Eve wiped water from her eyes, looking forward to getting back inside where it was dry and comfortable. The hem of her dress was covered in mud. It would have to be soaked, along with her muddy stockings.

A bolt of lightning cut across the sky, making the horse Eve was leading rear up on its hind legs. For a brief moment, she was terrified by the thrashing hooves. Then she remembered to keep calm, that nothing would happen to her as long as she remained calm and loving toward the animal.

Daed made a move toward them, as though to help her, but Eve held him off. It would only upset the horse more if he felt as though he were being surrounded.

"Peace, Clover! Peace! There, there." She ran a gentle hand over the horse's muzzle, scratching him behind the ears. Then she continued to lead him the extra hundred yards to the barn while her father closed the paddock gate.

"Eve, the nerve you have!" Daed laughed. "You might have missed your calling. A horse trainer might have been what you were meant to be!"

Eve blushed. She didn't think much of her accomplishment. She just seemed to know what the horse needed.

"Get back to the house," he said, frowning. "I do not want you to become ill, out in the storm this way. I disliked even having to ask you to help."

“That is what I am here for, Daed,” she said, smiling. “We work as a family, right?” She turned away and dared the walk back to the house. She didn’t run—it was pointless, as she was already soaked through. It was difficult enough to keep her footing, besides, in the slippery mud.

The rain had let up a bit, allowing Eve a better look around the land. Her family’s home wasn’t set far back from the road. And out there, just beyond the fence separating their land from the neighbors, was a pair of blinking lights.

Eve stopped, waiting to see if they would move. It seemed as though a car was stuck, perhaps in mud off the side of the road. Now the rain didn’t matter—it fell on her head, trickled down her face, but it was no matter. She wanted to see whether the driver would leave the car, stopped as it was by the big tree.

Daed and Caleb were still in the barn. Eve went alone to see whether the driver was in need of assistance—her father and brother were strong. Maybe they could push the car out of the mud. She ran to the road, slipping with every step.

When she reached the road, she saw a set of dark marks leading to where the car had settled. As though the driver lost control and the car spun. Eve ran to the car, now fearful. A man was slumped against the wheel, blood trickling down his head.

She looked up, screaming Caleb's name. When he appeared outside the barn, she screamed again. "He needs help!" She tried the door, pulling the handle, but it wouldn't budge.

Moments later, Daed and Caleb came on the run. They assessed the situation, trying all of the doors on the car. It took the two of them working in unison to pull the door beside the driver open.

Eve trotted behind them as they carried the man to the house. He was unconscious, his head still bleeding. They took him to the spare bedroom, laying him carefully down.

"See if he has other injuries," Eve fretted behind them.

"Wait outside," her father ordered. "We will check him over. I do not wish for you to see anything improper." Eve stood outside the room, frustrated. She had no desire to do anything except help the injured man. She listened while the two men checked his arms, legs, beneath his shirt for bleeding or bruising.

"He seems all right, come in." Eve returned. "There is a cut on his forehead, and a few additional scratches. No broken bones, it seems." Caleb stood back, pondering. He might have wounds inside, though, might he not?"

Daed nodded, grim. "Go down to the telephone shanty, Caleb. Call the hospital, ask for an ambulance. He should be looked at by a doctor."

Caleb left in a hurry. Eve saw him running for the road through the bedroom window. The rain was still coming down in buckets, the sky growing darker as night approached.

"I'll get towels, Daed. Some clothing from Caleb's room, maybe? He is shivering."

"Yes, do. I will change him. Caleb can help me when he returns." Eve dashed around the house, getting things together. She also poured hot water into a basin, to wash the man's forehead. There was blood all down the side of his face, too.

By the time she returned to the bedroom, Caleb was running up the stairs. He was winded, and bent at the waist to catch his breath.

"No…phone…lines are down." He panted for air.

"The phone isn't working?" Daed asked. Caleb shook his head.

"The lines have been brought down by the storm. I cannot reach the hospital. I don't believe an ambulance could make it here, even if I got through. Trees are blocking the road as far as the eye can see, in both directions."

The three of them stared at each other, then one by one they turned to the man in the bed.

Daed spoke up. "I suppose he will need to stay with us until we can make it through."

The Guest

Eve left the bedroom once again while Daed and Caleb dressed the man in dry clothing. He was nearly Caleb's size, so his clothing would fit near enough. While they worked, Eve changed out of her own wet clothing, setting her muddy dress to soak before returning with an oil lamp to the spare bedroom.

He was still unconscious. Eve sat by his side, placing a wash cloth in the water basin before applying the cloth to the stranger's face. There was a lot of dried blood, and Caleb had to empty the basin and refill it before everything was washed away. Then she sat, quiet. She wondered about him. Where had he come from? Where was he going when his car crashed?

"I suppose we should take shifts," Paul Lantz suggested. Eve looked up at her Daed, eyes wide.

"I will take the first shift," she said, almost out of instinct. It was part of her, the need to care for others. It was that need which had brought her to the stranger's car—the need to know whether there was any way to help the man.

He shook his head, his long beard shaking back and forth with him. “I don’t think that would be a wise idea, leaving you alone with a stranger—an Englischer, at that.”

Eve smiled. “I don’t think any harm will come to me. The man is unconscious. He can’t move, let alone assault me in any way.”

He laughed at her saucy tone. “Fair enough.”

“I will take the second shift,” Caleb offered. Eve promised to wake him in three hours, though she thought she might allow him to sleep a little longer. He needed the rest more than she did—everybody worked hard on a farm, but the labor of the men was more physically demanding. At least, Eve thought so. She did better with less sleep than her father or brother.

Once she was alone with him, Eve had the chance to think. Everything had happened so fast. Only an hour or so earlier, she was washing dishes and watching the storm. The storm still raged, but now she sat at the bedside of a sick man.

A sick man who happened to be very handsome.

Her cheeks flushed at the turn her thoughts had taken, but there was no denying them. With his face cleaned of blood, except for the little bit seeping through the bandage Eve applied once he was cleaned up, it was clear that he was a very nice looking man. He might have been the most handsome man she'd ever seen. There were a few nice looking young men in her community, one or two of whom she had stolen glances at during church meetings or gatherings. None of them held a candle to the stranger.

His eyes were closed, naturally, and his long, thick eyelashes fell on his cheeks. They seemed to go on forever. His jaw was firm, square. His nose was fine and straight. His hair was thick and dark, swept back from his forehead.

She looked at his eyes again, wishing they were open. Not only would that mean he was awake, naturally, but Eve would be able to see so much more of the person he was inside. It was so easy to tell what a person was like by looking into their eyes.

She wondered what color his eyes were, too.

Then, she shook herself. It was silly, having thoughts like these. Not only that, but they were bound to lead in a direction she knew she should not stray toward. She was thinking about him in a way she shouldn't think about any man, except the man she was to marry.

It was doubly wrong to think this way about an Englischer. He was from another world, far removed from the ways of the Amish like herself. His world was forbidden to her, full of temptation which would only serve to lead her away from Gott.

Still, it was nearly impossible not to be interested in him, to wish she could speak to him. All she had to do was sit by his bedside. Her mind wandered on its own.

Did he have girlfriends? She was sure he must, somebody as handsome as he was. There had to be plenty of girls all over him. She knew how free and easy girls behaved in the Englisch world. She couldn't even wear her blonde hair down in public, or leave it uncovered. Yes, the girls were probably crazy about him.

She told herself it wasn't wrong to have these thoughts, since the stranger was sick and unconscious. As long as they didn't go any further, she wouldn't have anything to feel guilty about.

He stirred fretfully. She leaned over him, placing a hand on his forehead to soothe him. She wanted to be sure he wasn't running a fever, too. She knew that some illnesses could lead to fever and infection if left unchecked. He was cool to the touch, and Eve thanked Gott for it. If he were badly injured inside, there would be nothing she could do for him.

He had a strong, fine body. It was unlikely that he worked on a farm, the way her brother did, though their builds were very much the same. He might have been an athlete. In any case, he was a very active person who took care of himself.

Not for the first time did she ask herself where he was supposed to be. She wondered if the people there were worried over him. She would have been, in their shoes, knowing he was on his way during a fierce storm. The rain still fell, and the wind had picked up. It made the windows rattle in their casements. She shuddered to think of the condition of the farm by the time the rain stopped. There would be a lot of work to do.

And there was him. The stranger. She wondered if he would be with them for very long. How long would it take before the roads were cleared? Daed and Caleb could take him to the hospital in the buggy if need be, if the telephone lines weren't up in time to call for an ambulance.

The Awakening

His eyes opened wide, sweeping from side to side to take in the room. It was a simple room, as every room in their home—or in any Amish home, for that matter. As it was the spare bedroom, there was no clothing hanging from the pegs on the wall. The room's furniture consisted of the bed on which he laid, a small table beside and the chair in which Eve sat. She was certain this was all strange to him. His own room must have been filled with so many things.

"Where am I?" he whispered, looking as though he were ready to spring from the bed. Eve moved reflexively, without giving any thought to whether or not it was proper to lean over him and place her hands on his arms. To her, in that moment, he wasn't a strange man. He was a person in need of care, who didn't know what was best for him. She did.

"There, there," she murmured, trying to calm him. "You must stay still. You have been injured."

"Injured? What happened to me? Where am I?" He looked at her, his eyes searching her face. "Who are you?"

"Please, lie back," she murmured. "Relax. I will tell you everything, but you must relax."

He hesitated, and Eve thought for a fleeting moment of how strong his arms felt beneath her hands. Instinct had fallen away, and now the truth of what she was doing flooded her thoughts and made her blush. She pulled her hands back as though his skin burned beneath them.

He didn't appear to notice her sudden change in demeanor, but did as she asked of him. Eve breathed a sigh of relief. It hadn't occurred to her that he might try to run away when he awoke. There was little chance of her keeping a grown man still, all alone.

"What happened to me?" he asked. "How am I injured?" Then, he raised a hand to his head. "Oh. My head hurts."

"I'm sure it does. I'm sorry we do not have anything to give you for it—painkillers, I mean. I do have aspirin, however." The bottle was beside him on the table, along with a glass of water. He took the pills gratefully, drinking the water in one long gulp.

"Do you remember losing control of your car?" Eve asked.

His eyes narrowed, as though he was trying to recall. "Is that what happened?" His voice was weak, confused. Eve wondered what he sounded like when he wasn't injured. Though it was just above a whisper, she heard the depth and warmth beneath the confusion. She thought his laugh was probably rich and deep.

"Yes. There was a terrible storm—well, it's still raining," she said, motioning toward the window. The rain fell steadily, though with less strength than before. "I found you in your car, crashed into a tree. You were on the road just in front of this house."

"That's where I am? In that house?" He smiled slightly. "I guess you're Amish, then. That explains a lot."

Eve blushed again. At least he was in good humor. Some Englischers behaved as though the Amish were something to be afraid of. As though something may rub off on them, a strangeness. How many times had she gone to town only to be ogled like an oddity?

"Yes, you're in an Amish household. Hence the oil lamp." She smiled self-deprecatingly, and was rewarded with a wider smile from her patient.

“I didn’t think it would be like this,” he murmured, looking around again.

“How did you think it would be?”

“I don’t know. Not like this. It’s so simple.”

“Plain,” Eve acknowledged. “It is what we strive for.”

He turned his head, taking in the measure of the small room. When he did, another pain must have struck him. His hand went to his head, where he touched his fingers to the bandage Eve had applied. “What’s this?”

“Your head was bleeding. I cleaned up the blood and bandaged it for you. It looks as though that was the extent of your injuries, though there’s no telling for sure. We could not get you to a hospital right away, as the storm made the roads impassable.”

“Oh. I see.” He frowned.

“Do you hurt anywhere else? Can you move everything?”

He tested himself out, moving his arms and legs, turning gingerly from side to side. He shrugged. “I think I’m all right.”

"Just the same, I think it would best if you stayed still. If you were to aggravate an injury, there would be no way for me to help you." She bit her lip, shuddering a little at the thought of feeling so helpless.

He smiled. "It looks like you've done a pretty good job so far."

Eve looked down at the quilt covering his legs, trying to hide a shy smile at his compliment. "Thank you."

"Can you tell me something?"

"Of course." She thought she knew what the question would be. How can you live this way? Don't you have any television? Radio? Computer? Don't you get bored?

Instead, he asked, "What's your name?"

Her relief was so complete, she almost laughed aloud. "Eve. Eve Lantz."

"Eve. What a beautiful name." He smiled softly.

"What's your name?" she asked, feeling shy again.

"Oliver Smith."

"A nice name, too," she smiled.

"How old are you?" he asked.

"I turned twenty last month."

"Twenty? You seem so much older."

She touched her face, self-conscious. "Do I look old to you?"

He laughed softly, and Eve felt her cheeks go red again. What was it about this young man that made her so quick to blush? "No," he replied. "I didn't mean it that way. You look just right for twenty. It's the way you act; the way you speak. It makes you seem more mature. That's all I meant to say."

Eve pushed aside the glow she felt inside when Oliver mentioned her looking "just right". Do not allow for flattery, she reminded herself. It was a slippery slope. Once she felt he was flattering her, she would become more attached to the idea that he had thoughts about her that were more than friendly. She had seen her best friend fall into such a trap with a boy she wished would court her. The littlest compliment and she thought for certain that he liked her. She'd been distraught when he started courting another girl, instead.

Besides, this wasn't a matter of a little fun at a singing. That was harmless, and with members of her community. Oliver was an Englischer. It was much more serious for her to allow her feelings to run away from her when a man like him was involved.

"What do you do, Eve? Do you go to school?"

She shook her head. "No, we do not go past eighth grade."

His blue eyes widened. "None of you?"

Eve shook her head. Oliver asked, "What if you want to be a doctor or something? Or a lawyer? Don't you have those?"

"No. Such learning…how do I explain? We believe that it's only for Gott to know everything."

"Gott? You mean God?" Eve nodded. "So you limit your education because of your faith?"

"You could put it that way, yes. Besides, our occupations are more…how do you say it? Hands on?" Oliver nodded with a smile. "So the boys go to work as apprentices. Carpentry, farming, that sort of thing. The girls learn to keep house."

"I can't imagine it," he said, softly. "Not that it's wrong or strange, just...different. Where I come from, the more educated you are, the better."

"Why?"

His mouth opened, then closed. He laughed. "I don't know! I mean, for some professions it makes sense. Being a doctor, for instance. I would want the smartest, most educated person possible. Right?"

"That does make sense."

"But sometimes..." he continued, "sometimes it feels like we're expected to be educated just because we're supposed to be. It's hard to explain. I know a lot of people who graduated with degrees but still didn't know what they wanted to do. Or their degree didn't really get them anything. Back in the day, if you went to college you could expect a decent job. That's not the case anymore. So some people to go graduate school to get a better degree, instead. That's what I'm doing now. I'm in business school."

"What kind of business?"

He chuckled softly. "I don't know yet. Just business. And when I'm finished, I'm going to have a lot of money to pay back. I borrowed the money for school. Almost everybody does now."

"We don't do that—borrow money, I mean. There's no such thing."

"I'm sure that makes life easier." He sighed. "I don't know how I'm going to pay them back. There are people I know who are ten years out of college who haven't paid them off yet. And they don't have the job they thought they'd have, anyway. Sometimes they work in completely different professions."

"So why go to school?"

He shrugged. "It's expected. It's all pretty complicated."

"It doesn't sound so complicated to me."

He smiled. "I guess it doesn't. Maybe I'm making it out to be more complicated than it is. There's a lot of conditioning that goes on in my world. I guess."

"Conditioning?"

"Being told that things have to be a certain way."

“I guess we have conditioning too, then. We are taught that Gott comes above all else. We serve Him, and we serve each other.”

“But that’s conditioning for a good cause, something that makes you feel good inside. You can believe in that.”

He seemed very troubled. Eve got the feeling he wasn’t very happy. He seemed very intelligent. Simply going through life without knowing why he did what he did wasn’t enough for him. Eve had never had that problem—not for lack of intelligence, but for lack of doubt. She had never once doubted her place in the world or whether the decisions she made were the right ones. She couldn’t imagine having such questions as the ones Oliver seemed to have.

She decided to change the subject to a topic she hoped was more pleasant for him. It was important to keep him calm and distracted from any pain he felt.

“Where were you going when you had your accident?”

He smiled. “Home, to see my family. Oh, jeez, I hope they’re not worried about me.” He looked around, then laid back with a sigh. “I guess you don’t have a phone.”

She shook her head. “I’m sorry, we don’t. There’s a telephone shanty down the road, but Caleb already went to it to call an ambulance for you. It isn’t working. The lines went down in the storm.”

“Who’s Caleb?”

“My brother. He ran out in the storm to see if he could call the hospital, and told us the lines were down and the road blocked by trees.”

Oliver sighed, staring at the ceiling. Then, his eyes lit up. “My cell. It was in my pocket.”

Eve excused herself, going downstairs to where Oliver’s clothing was hanging over the backs of the kitchen chairs to dry. In the pocket of his pants were a wallet, and a black rectangular piece of plastic. She knew it was a phone, having seen enough Englischers using them in town. It seemed as though they couldn’t live without them.

Carrying it gingerly, Eve returned to the spare bedroom. Oliver smiled when he saw how careful she was being. He thanked her, then swiped his fingers along the surface. It was a challenge, not staring in fascination. Eve had the feeling she should not observe too carefully. It was a temptation.

"It doesn't work," he said, tossing it onto the bed with a frustrated sigh. "There's no signal."

She didn't understand exactly what he meant, but there was no misunderstanding his disappointment. "I'm sorry. Hopefully, we'll be able to get you to a hospital tomorrow, and you can call from there."

"I hope so. They're probably pretty worried about me. I should have been there hours ago."

Eve frowned in sympathy. "I'm sorry. I'm sure it will be all right, once they hear from you."

"I guess." He still looked troubled.

"Tell me about your family," she said. "Where do you live?"

He grinned. "Quakertown. It's a nice place. Not as nice as this, though."

"Nice? What do you consider nice?"

"Quiet. Pretty. Peaceful. There are quiet areas, but not the sort of quiet you have here." Eve could understand what he meant. She loved the peace of a quiet morning or evening. It was so easy to talk to Gott, to feel His presence in her heart.

Oliver held up one hand to signal silence. Eve nearly held her breath in anticipation. The only sound around them was the rat-a-tat-tat of rain hitting the roof, the window, the walls. He smiled after a few moments. "You have no idea how nearly unnerving it is. Even when no one is speaking, where I come from, there's always sound coming from somewhere. A refrigerator motor, or a computer fan, or something. The only time it gets really quiet like this is when the power goes out…which I guess it has for a lot of people in town." He chuckled. "I guess that's one area where you have them beat. You can handle a storm better than they can!"

He had such a nice laugh—warm, rich, deep. It made Eve smile, even as it sent a tingle through her body. She wished she could hear it all the time.

Then she reminded herself that she was Oliver's caregiver. Nothing more. It was a bleak realization, but nonetheless true. Thinking about him in any other way would lead to nothing but disappointment when he left. Which he would, as soon as the roads were clear.

Easy Conversation

"So, Eve. You never did tell me what it is you do." Oliver waited with an expectant smile.

"I don't know what you mean by 'do'. I don't have an occupation, if that's what you mean. I work here, in the home." She shrugged.

"Is that enough for you?"

She furrowed her brow. "Shouldn't it be?"

"I'm not trying to be insulting," he said, stretching a bit on the bed. "Boy, I'm really starting to get sore."

She bit her lip, looking him up and down, switching into the mode of caregiver rather than simply a girl staring at a young man, wishing he would laugh for her again. "Do you have any difficulty breathing? Does anything hurt more than anything else?"

He shook his head. "I don't think you have to worry too much. I sort of remember the crash now. I saw the tree coming and I braced myself. I stiffened up. They say that's why drunk drivers sometimes walk away from a crash with no problems—they didn't stiffen up. They rolled with the motion of the car." Then it was his turn to blush, for once, his face reddening beneath his tanned complexion. "Sorry. You have no idea what I'm talking about. I'm rambling."

"I have some idea," she said. "It makes sense. Would you like a hot water bottle for anything in particular? Your back, maybe?"

"I think it will be all right," he said, shifting again. "It's too warm for a hot water bottle, anyway. That's one thing you could use in times like this. Air conditioning."

Eve agreed with that—the storm meant leaving the windows closed against the rain, and it was quite warm. She turned to open the window a crack, taking a chance. A breath of cooler air immediately flowed into the room.

Oliver smiled. "I love the air during a rain storm." Then he grew serious. "We never did talk about what is you do. You work in the home, then?"

"Yes."

"Do you have any conveniences? Like…I don't know…a washing machine?"

She grinned. "Yes. You'd be surprised at some of the things we have, though not nearly as fancy as Englischer versions."

"Englischer?" His brow furrowed.

"Jah, Englischer." She pointed to him.

"I see." He grinned.

"I do not have a clothes dryer, though. We use the sun." She smiled. "We have a refrigerator in the kitchen, and a stove which runs on gas. We're lucky. Some of the more conservative orders do not allow for such things."

"Luxurious." He said it with a kind smile. It seemed as though he found everything amusing—but he wasn't making fun. "My mom couldn't live without her dishwasher and dryer and hairdryer and curling iron and blender and…the list goes on and on."

"When you're raised without such things, you don't know what life is like with them. So you can't miss them." She shrugged. "It's really simple when you look at it that way."

"I'm sure you're right. I bet your mom probably cooks better than my mom without all the fancy appliances."

Eve bit her lip, cast her eyes down at the floor. "Did I say something wrong?" he asked, strain touching his voice.

She shook her head. "It's all right. It's just that my Mamm...she passed on, two years ago."

"Oh, I'm so sorry."

Eve nodded, and waited until the tightness in her throat eased a bit before speaking. "She had cancer. She wasn't sick for very long—not very long that we knew, anyway."

"That's awful. I'm really sorry to hear it."

"We were very close," Eve whispered. "I took care of her, until she left us."

Oliver was quiet for a long time, seeming to take it all in. Finally, he spoke. "She was blessed to have you with her in the end. In my world...well, a lot of people don't get that luxury."

"It was a blessing to me," Eve insisted. "It was the least I could do for her. She had already done so much for me."

"That can't have been easy. Losing her, or taking over the household in her place."

"Losing her wasn't easy. It's still not easy. But taking over the work wasn't very difficult for me. I learned from an early age." She quickly wiped her cheeks with her hands, catching a few stray tears, then raised her head. "I always wanted to know how to do the cooking and cleaning and mending."

"It came naturally to you, then."

"That sort of thing does. I enjoy it. Taking care of the people I care for." Then her cheeks burned hot, and she looked away again. She didn't wish to give him any ideas as to why she was sitting up with him. Of course, part of it was the easy conversation they created together, and the way he seemed fascinated with all the aspects of Eve's life. And the way she was fascinated by him, by his curiosity and his warmth and the way he accepted an answer without judgment or skepticism, like so many Englischers did.

The rest was her desire to make sure he recovered. She reminded herself that this was her main reason in sitting up with him for so long.

When she met his blue eyes again, they twinkled in the light from the oil lamp. "You're a very good person. I sensed that right away, when I first woke up. You have a gentle heart. It's easy to talk to you. Am I asking too many questions?"

"No, not at all. I like the chance to talk about my life. I don't get it often. And if I'm ever asked questions, they're usually much more prying and skeptical. I don't know how to explain it any better."

Oliver seemed to understand. He was good at understanding what she meant. "They're nosy and rude, in other words."

She giggled. "In other words."

"Yeah. We're all raised so differently from you, it's unimaginable that you live like you do. But now that I'm here, I get it. A little bit, anyway."

"It's not so different in a lot of ways," Eve insisted. "I mean, I guess. I've never known an Englischer before. But doesn't it seem to make sense that we wouldn't be so different? We all want the same things. We all feel the same things."

"You're right. It just looks different on the outside." He smiled gently, and Eve knew he understood. He wasn't just pretending to understand or trying to be nice. He seemed to really hear what she was saying. And he was so handsome when he smiled, and the dimples appeared in his cheeks.

It doesn't matter that he's handsome. It doesn't matter. She reminded herself time and again, but it didn't seem to matter. The longer she spent with him, the harder it was to keep herself from thinking of him as a man—not just a patient. She knew this meant she should leave him alone…but she couldn't imagine dragging herself from his bedside. Not when there was so much more they could be talking about. It felt natural, sitting here, telling stories in the flickering light from the lamp. She'd never had a more rapt audience.

She told him about the traditions of her Ordung. The way members of the community always looked out for one another. He seemed amazed by that, while to Eve it was a matter of fact. She told him of barn raisings and other gatherings, of the food the women prepared for these gatherings. He asked about church, and whether she attended. She explained their church services, how they took place at the homes of the community members. "When it is our turn, we host the community in our home."

"What about social activities? Do you have any of those?"

"We have singings. Girls and boys get together, often after church meetings, to sing songs. It's our way of spending time together."

"That's it? No parties or anything?"

"We might celebrate a birthday, or something like that. But no, we don't throw parties for the sake of throwing parties." She smiled at his surprise. "The adults know it's important for us to have fun together and, you know, see each other."

Now he was smiling. "You mean checking each other out?"

"Checking out?"

Oliver laughed softly. "You know. Seeing who you like." There was something new to his tone of voice, now. He wasn't just asking out of curiosity. There was something else there.

Now Eve's cheeks burned hotter than ever. How had their conversation taken this turn? "Yes. That was what I meant. Since we don't have school or other activities, it's our way of...checking each other out."

"I guess there has to be a way. Or else how would you find the person you wanted to marry?"

Eve couldn't bring herself to raise her eyes. She was afraid he would see everything she was feeling, written plainly on her face. That was one thing about her—she was never any good at hiding her feelings.

"Is there anyone you're…checking out?" he asked, softly.

"You mean courting?" she asked.

"Courting? Is that what you call dating? So you do have that?"

"Yes—though I'm sure it's very, very different to what you're used to."

"It probably is." She wasn't looking at him, examining her lap instead, but she heard the humor in his voice. Again, he wasn't making fun. He didn't think she was backward or strange. He was only making an observation. There was no mistaking the fact that he was deeply, genuinely interested.

"Thank you for taking the time to talk with me," he said. "I might have gone nuts, lying here with nobody to talk to. And when would I ever get the opportunity to learn everything I've learned tonight?"

"All you had to do was crash your car," she murmured with a smile.

He laughed, then winced. "Sometimes it hurts a lot," he muttered, holding his hand to his head.

Eve leaned over him, checking his bandage. There was still a bit of blood seeping from his wound, but not much. "I've kept you talking for far too long," she said, admonishing herself. He needed to rest, while she indulged her growing attraction to him by prattling on and on and her life. It was selfish.

"Please, not at all," he said. He touched her hand, where it taped the gauze bandage back to his forehead. "You don't know how much I've enjoyed talking with you. It's been a rare treat."

His touch took her breath away. All at once she was nearly giddy with excitement. Something strange and special was happening.

It was also ill-advised. She pulled her hand away, as though he burned. "It was nothing," she said. "The least I could do. And I don't get the chance to talk much, not with someone so kind."

He settled back onto the pillows with a grimace. "What a headache. I don't think I've ever had such a headache before."

"You should try to sleep," Eve said. "I'll leave you, so you can."

"No—please, don't. I don't think I could sleep anyway," he said. "Though I'm keeping you from your sleep. That's selfish of me."

She bit her lip, thinking. "You know, I remember when I was little and I couldn't sleep because I was sick. Mamm would sing to me, and it always relaxed me. She would tell me to close my eyes and picture the things she was singing about. And when I did, before I knew it, I was dreaming about them. It always worked."

"Will you sing to me?"

"I could, if you think it will help you." It was embarrassing, the thought of singing an old lullaby to a grown man—an Englischer, at that. But her job was to take care of him, and that meant helping him sleep.

"All right. Let's see." She cleared her throat. "Now, close your eyes."

He closed them with a smile.

Eve sang in English, since he would understand it, though her mother had always sung to her in Pennsylvania Deitsch.

Sleep, my baby, sleep!
Your Daddy's tending the sheep.
Your Mommy's taken the cows away.
Won't come home till break of day.
Sleep, my baby, sleep!

Sleep, my baby, sleep!
Your Daddy's tending the sheep.
Your Mommy's tending the little ones,
Baby sleep as long as he wants.
Sleep, my baby, sleep!

Sleep, my baby, sleep!
Your Daddy's tending the sheep.
Your Mommy is cooking Schnitz today,
Daddy's keeping the bugs away!
Sleep, my baby, sleep!

Sleep, my baby, sleep!
Your Daddy's tending the sheep.
Your Mommy's gone off on a gossiping flight,
And won't be back till late tonight!
Sleep, my baby, sleep!

Sleep, my baby, sleep!
Your Daddy's tending the sheep.
Your Mommy's tending the white cows –

They keep a very manury house!
Sleep, my baby, sleep!

By the time she finished the lullaby, Oliver's breathing had slowed. When the last notes left her mouth, he didn't stir. She waited, wondering if he were really asleep again. After a few minutes, it looked as though he was.

She watched him for a few minutes as he slept. He was so handsome, just as she had noted before—though he seemed even more so, now that they had spent so much time talking together. He had a special sort of charm, a warmth and sincerity which made even the plainest man or woman more attractive.

For the first time in her life, Eve wished she wasn't Amish.

When the thought rang in her head, her eyes opened wide. This was wrong. She had to leave him alone. He was leading her thoughts astray. Why should she wish to not be Amish, when it was the life she loved? Because of a stranger? One who would leave her life as soon as the roads were clear?

Her heart was heavy, her mind in a daze. She stood quickly, quietly, taking the lamp with her. It was far too tempting to stay with him. She made a hasty retreat to her bedroom, checking the small clock on the table beside her bed when she did. It was after one in the morning. She'd have to be up in only a few hours.

Climbing into bed, Eve said a fervent prayer to be forgiven for her thoughts. It was a moment of weakness, caused by the lateness of the hour. She wouldn't let herself be led astray.

Time to Leave

The following morning, Eve woke with a song in her heart. It had only been a few hours, but she felt well-rested. She knew Gott forgave her for the weak, silly thought she'd had before going to bed. She had only been tired and worn out. What was important was making sure Oliver was still resting comfortably, then tending to Daed and Caleb as she did every morning. She dressed quickly, then went in to check on him.

He was fast asleep. He probably needs it, she thought to herself. A gentle hand on his forehead told her he was still cool, no fever. She gave a silent prayer of thanks for that, then went to the kitchen to start breakfast for her father and brother.

"How is your patient?" Caleb asked, meeting her a short while later.

"Sleeping," she said with a smile. "He seems well. I spoke with him for a long time during the night."

He raised an eyebrow. "You should have called me."

"All was well," she assured him. "We only spoke of our lives. You know. His family, my family. He asked many questions about the way we live."

Caleb took a cup of coffee, rolling his eyes. "Aren't you used to those questions by now?"

"No, it wasn't like that at all. He was genuine. Very kind. There was no judgment or discomfort." It was difficult to explain. There was a difference between a question asked out of curiosity and one asked out of judgment. She had been asked many uncomfortable questions before, by random strangers in town who felt it acceptable to approach her while in line and ask how she lived without electricity or the internet.

"I'll go check on the telephone after chores are finished, and I'll ask around about the roads."

"Thank you," Eve said. She put out platters of eggs, sausage, potatoes, and biscuits. Her Daed came down moments later to eat heartily before it was time to milk the cows and tend to the horses. He asked questions similar to those Caleb asked. She reminded herself that nothing improper had gone on between them, so there was nothing to be ashamed of.

Oliver slept until midday, when Eve was just setting out dinner. Fried chicken, buttered noodles, pickled vegetables, fresh bread and apple butter. Dessert was shoofly pie, her father's favorite. As she set out the last plate, she heard footsteps on the stairs.

"Oliver!" She rushed to the stairs, intent on helping him down.

"I'm all right," he said. "I promise. The smell of the food drew me down."

"I would have brought some up to you!" she said, giving him a comfortable seat. "You shouldn't be on your feet."

"I'm really fine. My head still hurts, and I'm sore in a lot of places, but I think I'll be okay." He was dressed in his own clothing; which Eve had left in the bedroom for him. The t-shirt showed off his strong physique. Eve averted her eyes after helping him sit

"Just the same, you should take it easy." She went out to the front porch, calling the men in for their meal. There was no denying the way her heart raced at Oliver's presence, and a breath of fresh air was needed to cool herself. The rain-washed air was sweet and comfortable in comparison to the previous day's sticky humidity.

When they came in, Paul and Caleb had questions for Oliver. Caleb told him the telephone lines were still down, but the roads were cleared thanks to the combined efforts of Amish and Englischers.

"We can take you the hospital in our buggy," Paul said.

Eve's heart clenched. She knew it was for the best. Oliver needed real care. He might have had a brain injury, even though it didn't seem as though he did. Old Jonah Stoltzfus had been injured in an accident years before, when Eve was young, after falling from a ladder. He had seemed all right and refused care, only to be rushed to the Englischer hospital days later with excruciating head pain. He passed away there. The doctor said he had suffered an injury to the brain when he fell. Eve shuddered to think of Oliver facing the same outcome.

Still, the thought of him leaving was unbearable. After only one night. There was an attachment she couldn't name—one which she knew was unsuitable, and dangerous. He wasn't from her world. He knew nothing of her faith, of the way she lived. It was forbidden to have a relationship with an Englischer. And yet, for the first time in her life, Eve felt temptation. She knew she would miss him when he was gone. He added to her life simply by being in the same room.

He appreciated her cooking, too. "You have your appetite. That's a good sign," Eve joked.

"Even if I didn't, I couldn't resist this chicken. Easily the best I've ever had." He grinned at her, then took another drumstick. She looked down at the table to hide her proud smile. She felt Caleb's keen eyes on her and deliberately avoided them. She thought he might have additional questions for her once their guest left.

And leave, he did. It was inevitable. Once the meal was over—Eve admitted to herself that she tried to stretch it out longer than was necessary—Caleb pulled the buggy around to the front of the house.

Eve wondered if it was possible for a heart to actually break. She felt as though hers was. How was it possible to feel so attached to him? She watched him walk out to the buggy, fighting against the sadness blooming inside her.

He turned at the last minute, returning to where she stood on the steps. "Thank you for taking care of me," he said, smiling warmly. The dimples appeared in his cheeks, and Eve's heart skipped a beat.

"It was nothing," she said, waving a self-deprecating hand.

"Not at all. It was really something. You didn't have to sit up with me and talk to me. You didn't even have to find me. I think it was part of His plan." Oliver looked up at the sky, then back to her. He winked, taking her breath away. Was there any end to his charm?

"I'm sure it was," she murmured.

"I'll keep in touch—I promise." He smiled again, looking as though he wanted to shake her hand or touch her in some way but holding back. He climbed into the buggy, flanked by Caleb and Eve's father, and they drove away. She watched with a wistful heart until the buggy was only a dot on the horizon.

She wondered whether he would, in fact, keep in touch with her.

***

Hours later, the buggy returned. Oliver was gone, of course.

Eve ran out the door to meet them. "How was he?" she asked, peppering them with questions before the buggy had even come to a complete stop. "Did you stay to find out? Did he manage to call his family?"

Caleb looked amused, but said nothing. Her Daed held up a patient hand.

"He will be fine," he said. "He needed several stitches for the cut on his head, and medicine for the pain. The doctor assured him after performing tests that he would be all right. The car will be picked up by a garage later today, though he is advised not to drive. His parents are on their way to get him now."

Eve knew this was as thorough a report as she would get. She sighed softly, nodding her head. It was for the best. She was glad he was as well as could be, too.

He must have seen the concern on his daughter's face. "It's so good of you to care so much, as always," he said. "Your mother always said you had the biggest heart of anyone she'd ever known, and she was right. Our Englischer friend was lucky to have crashed here, where someone like you could take care of him."

Eve smiled as her father kissed her cheek, then went about his work. She went to the garden to see what could be salvaged. It would be helpful to keep her mind and hands busy. The less time she had to brood over Oliver, the better.

The storm had done some damage, but not as much as Eve had imagined. She straightened the tomato cages, the trellises on which the green bean, cucumber and summer squash vines climbed. It didn't seem as though anything was ruined or drowned. She thanked Gott for that—she'd spent a lot of time in her garden, nursing the vegetables. The produce from it kept them eating throughout summer, then through autumn and winter once Eve did the canning. Her next trip would be to the orchard, to check the fruit trees. They grew apples, peaches, pears and plums. The apples weren't ready yet, of course, but the other fruit was coming along. Eve was happy to see that it was still doing well—only a few limbs had been lost to the storm and some of the fruit tossed to the ground, but the tress still stood.

All of this, and the rest of her chores, were done in a haze. She felt numb, almost, as though nothing could get through to her. All she could think about was him. Had his family arrived yet? Was he on his way home? How did he feel? Would he remember her?

That was the biggest question, the one which weighed heaviest. Would he remember her? And if he did, would it be only as some shy, awkward Amish girl? Some oddity? A person he would never have been able to meet otherwise, and one who was so totally removed from his sphere of experience that he would brush her off as inconsequential? Would she become a joke to him over time, as so many Englischers considered the Amish to be?

She couldn't believe she would, no matter how dark and troubled her thoughts were. He was a kind, considerate person. He had a good heart. He wouldn't discount her.

Would he keep in touch? Or was he only saying it as a way of thanking her?

The Right Path

A week passed, and Eve's thoughts were no less with Oliver than they had been in the first moments after he left her porch. He had gone back to his regular life by then, of course, and was probably too busy thinking about himself and the distractions around him to remember the shy, quiet girl who nursed him through a stormy night.

She hung the wash one day, sighing loudly as she did. Even the chores she normally enjoyed were drudgery to her, thanks to her troubled heart. And hanging wash was always something she'd liked to do. Watching the sheets billow in the breeze, smelling the sunshine that seeped into the cotton. She enjoyed being outdoors, too, and it was a beautiful day. Nothing seemed to get through to her, though. She felt strangely detached.

"Still thinking about your Englischer?"

Eve whirled around, gasping in surprise. Her best friend, Martha, laughed at her reaction.

"Martha! You startled me!" Eve giggled, putting a hand over her racing heart.

“I only said your name three times before you finally heard me,” Martha replied with a smirk. “I finished my chores early and thought I would come over to see if you needed help.”

Eve smiled at her friend’s thoughtfulness. Martha always made it a point to visit Eve when she had the chance. Running an entire household was a lot of work—Martha had three sisters to help their Mamm with the work, while Eve was alone. She offered her assistance whenever she could.

“You can help me hang the sheets,” Eve said. “Then we can sit for a while. I would like to take a rest before starting dinner. Your timing is perfect.”

The girls worked cheerfully, laughing over a story Martha told about some mischief her baby brother had gotten into. “He won’t try to jump from the barn into a haystack ever again! Mamm nearly fell over when she saw him do it.”

Eve giggled. “I’ll never understand why little boys do things like that. It’s so much easier being a girl. We don’t dare each other to nearly break our necks.”

“No, but we’re the ones who tend to the boys when they go through with a dare.” Martha shook her head. "Jacob and Nathaniel were both punished for daring him, too. Daed was furious with them."

"I think it's an older brother's job to torment the younger ones. I'm glad I'm the oldest—Caleb was enough trouble as a little brother. If he were older?" Eve rolled her eyes.

The two girls sat on the steps of the house, basking in the sunlight. Eve sighed. She would normally have soaked up the sun with a smile, and enjoyed looking out over the fields with their rows and rows of cornstalks. She would have enjoyed the knowledge that autumn was coming—it was her favorite time of the year, as much as she enjoyed spring and summer. Autumn was so crisp and cheerful, so beautiful when the trees changed color and the pumpkins and squash meant plenty of pies, soups, stews and other comforting foods.

None of it mattered, and it frustrated her. Why couldn't she enjoy life anymore? Her joys had always come from the simplest of things, but even that which always brought a smile to her face left her feeling flat and dull. Even her smiles were forced sometimes.

"What's the matter?" Martha asked, elbowing her. "Where were your thoughts when I first came over?"

Eve had told Martha all about Oliver, since she had to tell somebody or else she would have burst. She and Martha had no secrets from each other. They had been the closest of friends nearly since birth, their birthdays only three days apart.

"You know where they were," Eve grudgingly admitted. "You said it yourself."

"Eve. You know it's not right."

"I know! Believe me, if I didn't know, it wouldn't be so hard to keep wanting him to write to me. I do. Oh, Martha, there were so many things we felt the same about. I felt it. He wasn't happy in his world. He appreciates what we have, here. I know that if we wrote to one another, I could…I don't know…help him, somehow. It's so hard to explain."

"Eve, it isn't your job to help everybody," Martha pointed out. "You're always trying to take care of everyone. You look after your Daed and your brother. You take care of the sick people around the community. You nurse the animals when they're sick. It never ends."

"I can't help it."

Martha smiled lovingly. "I know. It's who you are. But this Englischer isn't the same as everyone else. He's an outsider. If he needs help understanding his life, it's not your place to help him through that. I'm sure he has a pastor or somebody he can talk to, if he's really that dissatisfied. It's up to him to figure things out."

Eve bit her lip, resting her chin in her palm. "I know."

"So why do you really want him to write to you, then? You can be honest with me, you know."

"You seem to know so much, why don't you tell me?" Eve replied tartly.

"Because you like him."

"Of course, because I like him." Eve buried her face in her hands. "I like him so much." She felt Martha's hand on her back.

"It's easy to get wrapped up when you're taking care of somebody, I guess," Martha mused. "You nurse them, and you care so much about whether they heal. I don't think you can be blamed for developing feelings for him."

"Oh, it's not just that. I guess that's part of it, though." Eve raised her head, staring glumly out across the green grass, to the tree where Oliver's car had crashed. The tree was scarred where the car had struck it. "It was more the way he understood me. He was the kindest, most respectful person. Genuinely kind, not pretend. And he was smart, and funny. He had the nicest laugh, and the bluest eyes."

Martha sighed. "But he was an Englischer, first and foremost."

"What difference does it make? Why can't we be friends?"

"Because you can't be friends with him. You care too much for him. It would be unwise. Besides...he hasn't written yet, has he?"

"You know he hasn't. I would have told you if he had."

"Then there's your answer. I don't want to be mean, but it's for the best. You would only be unhappier in the end if he did write to you, and you continued a friendship that way. You would grow more attached. Right?"

"Right. I know you're right, in my head at least. But my heart doesn't care." Even

Martha didn't understand. Eve always appreciated her friend's level head, but in the moment she wished Martha didn't always have to provide the voice of reason.

"Pray. Pray hard for strength. If Gott wanted to the two of you to be together, he would have made Oliver Amish…or you Englisch. It's not meant to be. You helped him, you might even have saved his life—who knows? You were put in his path for a reason. Gott knows best, right? But that reason…it's over. Your paths have split again. That's how life goes." She stood, hugging her friend. "Take it easy on yourself, and try to stop thinking about him. It only makes things harder, when you can't let go."

After her friend had left and she was alone again, Eve considered the advice she'd been given. Martha was always wise beyond her years—if Eve was a born caregiver, Martha was a born sage. She always gave the best advice, and it was almost always right.

Still, as she said to Martha, her heart didn't agree. Her mind knew the truth of Martha's words. It wasn't right to continue thinking about Oliver. It had been a week, an entire week. So much could happen. He had never even told her whether or not he had a girlfriend. He probably did, as handsome as he was. He'd gone back to her, and his life was moving on. His path led in another direction.

It seemed so unfair, to be given a taste of something special only to have it then taken away so quickly. There had been something special between her and Oliver, and no one could convince her otherwise. He wasn't like the others, who stared and whispered behind their hands. He didn't ask questions to be nosy and rude, the way he put it. he wanted to know more about her, and her life. He must have been genuinely interested.

For once, she hadn't felt like an anonymous Amish face in a crowd. She had felt seen, really seen. He made her feel worthy of attention and respect. It wasn't Amish to seek attention, but the attention he gave her wasn't a vain, proud attention. It was the sort of attention one person gives to another when they value their thoughts and opinions. He'd asked questions and listened to the answers. He hadn't judged her or the people in her community.

Why did he have to be so nice? Why did he have to be so handsome? Even if he'd been mean and ugly, she still would have cared for him until he could make it to the hospital—but at least then she could have forgotten about him. By now she would be turning her thoughts to the upcoming harvesting and canning she would do in preparation for the cold months. Her thoughts wouldn't be drifting off over and over to a man who had likely forgotten all about her.

Please, Gott, she prayed. Give me the strength to get back on the right path. Remove him from my heart, and let me be more open to the path you've laid out for me.

The Return

More time passed, as it always seemed to do. Days went by just as they always did before the fateful night of the big storm. People still talked about the storm—a lot of damage had been done to many homes and farms in the community. As Oliver had joked that night, the Amish had one advantage over the Englischers at such times: no reliance on electricity. Life went on more smoothly in a shorter amount of time for Eve and her family.

The concerns of daily life crowded in, as they seemed to do as well. Caleb caught a summer cold and was ill for nearly a week, during which time Eve tended to him while helping her Daed whenever she could. There were church meetings, and singings. Martha was courting with Samuel Fisher, which was very exciting. She would often come over to help Eve with chores and spend hours going on about him. Eve was happy to lend an ear, since Martha had been so patient with her in the past.

In all, life went back to normal. It was as though the storm never happened.

One thing didn't go back to normal, however. Eve's heart was just as troubled as ever. Summer turned to autumn, the days growing shorter and cooler. There was so much work to be done, with canning and preserving being at the top of Eve's list. She made short order of the summer crop, preparing it to be enjoyed all winter long. Yet even with all this, part of her mind was always on Oliver.

She could be mending a shirt or shelling peas, scrubbing a floor or kneading dough, and her thoughts would stray to him. What was he doing? What would he think of what she was doing? Did he ever think of her at all? Or had he forgotten all about her?

It was doubtless he had forgotten. After all, he lived in a fast-paced world, filled with activities and distractions. No matter that he had expressed a desire to live a different life—the minute he returned, she had left his mind.

That was the way it had to be, wasn't it? They were from two different worlds. There was no way for them to be anything more than passing acquaintances. Gott had not put him in her path for a future. He had been sent to her so she could help him until it was time for him to go to hospital. That was all. She had done her role as Gott set it in front of her.

It was long past time to move on. But how could she?

Eve prayed to Gott every day for the strength and grace to move on with her life. All this thinking and dreaming led down a path to unhappiness, dissatisfaction. Sure, it was nice enough when she was lost in reverie. Sometimes she would look out the window and imagine him walking toward her, up the path or from the fields. At those times she would smile and allow herself to get a little lost in the daydream. When she shook herself from it, her heart would be a little heavier than it was before. He wasn't there. He would never be there.

"What is it, Eve?" Caleb's eye, shrewd as always, caught sight of her sadness one day while bringing in firewood. A chill had come into the air, and Eve pulled a sweater over her dress and apron before helping her brother stack neatly chopping logs against the wall.

"What do you mean?"

"You seem so low lately. There's a melancholy to you. You're usually so cheerful. Are you feeling ill?"

She shook her head, telling herself to put on a smile. It wouldn't do to reveal her feelings to anyone else. They wouldn't understand—they hadn't spent time with Oliver, the way she had. He was merely an Englischer to them, nothing more. And Englischers were to be mistrusted, left alone to their own devices.

"Not at all," she said, smiling. She didn't feel the smile in her heart, though, and she knew it didn't reach her eyes.

"Eve." Caleb took her hand, holding her still. "This is me. I know you. Tell me the truth."

"I tell you, it's nothing." She pulled her hand away, trying to be lighthearted. "You're making something out of nothing. Let it be."

"Is it the Englischer? Oliver?"

His question took her breath away. She balled up her fists, hidden in the sleeve of her sweater, in an effort to maintain her composure. Just hearing his name caused her heart to clench.

"What makes you ask that?" She turned her back to her brother, busying herself at the sink. She didn't want him to see the look on her face.

"You haven't been the same since he was here. You're always so far away. Sometimes I have to say your name two, three times to get your attention. You were never like that before."

She shrugged. "Maybe I should have my hearing checked."

"Eve. Stop." He stood beside her, staying there until she turned with a sigh to face him. "It's all right to admit you think about him."

"No, it isn't. He's not one of us. And thinking about him only makes me feel worse." She sighed, wringing a dishcloth in her hands.

"What about any of the men in the community? I'm sure there must be someone here who is a better match for you." His fair skin turned pink. "I shouldn't be talking about things like this with my sister."

Eve laughed, swatting him with the dishcloth. "You're probably right. I appreciate your concern, though. And I'm trying. I really am. I pray every day for the strength to go on without these thoughts. I want to go back to the way things were before. I was happy then."

"You can be happy again. At the next singing, try to pay more attention to the others. All right. That's all I can say, now." He ducked out, embarrassed. Eve laughed again at his shyness.

He was right, though. She should focus her thoughts on the young men of her Ordung. There were many her age or somewhat older, all of whom were devoted to Gott. They would make good husbands. They might be able to help her heal her bruised heart.

***

One day in mid-October, Eve sat by the fire with her sewing in hand. Her father had managed to tear a hole in one of his shirts, though it was fortunate that the tear occurred along a seam.

Sewing was always relaxing for her, and she allowed her mind to wander while she did it. She remembered how she used to love sitting with her Mamm, spending hours by the fire. Her mother had taught her everything she knew about sewing—about housekeeping in general. Whenever she did something just as her mother did it, whether it was sewing a hem or baking bread or using a certain trick to get even the dirtiest work clothes clean, she thought of her.

Hard to believe it had been more than two years since her passing. What would she think of the woman Eve was becoming—had become? For she was a woman. Some of the girls she grew up with were already married, settling down into new lives with their new husbands. Eve envied them, though she knew envy was a sin. She wished it could be her. Maybe her day would come, eventually.

She had taken Caleb's advice to heart and turned her attention to the young men in the community, in a conscious effort to remove Oliver's presence from her mind. She left her heart open, reminding herself that it was not her will but Gott's which should be followed. When the right person came along, she would know. All she could do was pay attention to what Gott whispered to her.

She sighed. What would Mamm say, if she knew of all of this? Eve wasn't sure she would have told her mother what was in her heart, but if she had she knew her loving, gentle mother would have given sage advice. She was always so wise.

Eve wished for some of that wisdom. Gott, she prayed, please give me the strength to walk along the path you have chosen for me, and the wisdom to be happy no matter what that path may be.

Moments later, there was a soft knock at the door. As she was alone, the men working in the barn, she answered.

Her heart soared when the bluest pair of eyes stared into her own. She hadn't forgotten those eyes, not for a minute.

"Oliver!" She was breathless, giddy. Her heart was racing, her palms clammy. "What are you doing here?" Immediately she wondered if she looked all right, then reminded herself it didn't matter. Besides, he had seen her looking this way before, in her simple dress, the kapp pinned firmly over her coil of blonde hair.

"I came to see you," he said, softly. "I'm sorry for not having come sooner."

He looked so much the same, as though he'd only walked away from her moments earlier. The same smile, the same dimples, the same square jaw and dark hair, brushed back from his forehead. It was almost too much to be believed.

When she found her voice, Eve gave a quiet laugh. “I didn’t expect you to come at all.”

“I said I would keep in touch, though.”

“I know,” she murmured softly. “But I didn’t expect that you would.”

They stood there for a long while, him on the porch while she stood at the kitchen door. It wouldn’t be appropriate to invite him in, unchaperoned. Her father would be thunderously angry if he came in to find an Englischer visiting, even if it was Oliver.

“Let me get my coat,” she said, reaching for the coat on the hook, shoving her arms into it while her heart fluttered like an excited bird. Why had he come? It was enough to simply see him. He hadn’t forgotten her, after all. She knew an excited blush touched her cheeks, and while his back was turned she smoothed down the bit of hair visible outside her kapp.

Then, she took a deep breath. He was only there to thank her for helping him. She reminded herself that it had been many weeks since he stayed with them, and that she hadn’t heard from him once. She couldn’t mean that much to him if he was able to disappear the way he had. The thought centered and calmed her.

She stepped out onto the porch. It was late afternoon, and the sun was going down in a blaze of gold and red, the special sort of sunset that only occurred in autumn. In it, Oliver's healthy, tanned complexion glowed bronze. Though she had only just reminded herself that there was nothing between them, she couldn't keep her heart from skipping a beat when she noticed how indescribably handsome he was.

"It's good to see you, Oliver." It was the only thing she could think to say, but it came straight from her heart.

"It's been too long," he replied. It felt as though she was living in a dream. Was he really there, and sounding as though he were truly happy to see her? It was simply amazing.

"It has been a long time," she agreed, "but life goes on. I understand." She wanted to tell him how much she had missed him, and how strange it felt to miss someone who she'd only known for a short time. Only one evening spent talking, and he had worked his way into her heart.

“You look sad,” he observed. “I don’t remember seeing sadness in your eyes when we met. I hope I’m not the reason for it.”

There was so much in Eve’s heart, she didn’t know where to begin—or even whether she should. Was it wise to open herself up to him? Should she tell him how she felt? He had come back, after all. And he seemed pensive, as though something was on his mind. Had he been fighting the same feelings she’d been wrestling with ever since the day he left?

She felt strongly drawn to him, as though there was no choice but to be honest. It was so dangerous, though, admitting such feelings to an Englischer. *Please, Gott. Tell me what to do.*

When she didn’t answer, Oliver continued. “I hope you didn’t think that just because I didn’t come back, I wasn’t thinking about you.”

A spark of hope kindled inside Eve’s heart. “You were thinking about me?”

“Almost all the time,” he admitted, with a shy smile. “I hope you don’t think I’m being too forward or anything.”

"No!" She nearly shouted it, and her cheeks burned hot. He laughed.

"Well, that's good." His eyes twinkled and shone. Eve had almost forgotten how blue they were. "You see," he continued, "I didn't want to come back to see you until I was sure about what I was thinking. I knew I owed it to you to be absolutely sure."

"What were you thinking about?"

He shoved his hands deep in the pockets of his jacket, rocking back and forth on the balls of his feet. "It's not a decision I'm making lightly. I want you to know that. I've done a lot of soul searching, and I've talked it over with my family and a few of my friends. They all respect my decision, even if they don't necessarily understand it."

"What decision, though?"

He let out a shaky sigh. "I've decided to join the Amish faith."

Eve was rocked to her core. For a moment, it felt as though she shut down completely. She couldn't think. She could only feel. It was as though her every wish was coming true. Could it be a dream? "You mean it? Can you...just do that? So easily?"

Oliver laughed softly, shaking his head. "It's not easy. I mean, not just an overnight decision. And your bishop has spoken with me at great length on what it is I must do to prepare."

"You've spoken to the bishop?" Her voice was practically a squeak. She couldn't have been more surprised if she tried.

"Oh, sure!" He laughed his deep, rich laugh. "We've spent a lot of time together—I'm just coming from his home now, actually."

"Oliver…this is wonderful news! I know you can be happy here, among us. I knew there was something special about you, especially since you seemed so genuinely interested in our faith. Only…"

"Only?"

It was difficult for Eve to get the words out, but she needed to know. "Are you sure you are joining us because you're running toward something, or because you're running away from something else?"

"You know, that's exactly one of the questions the bishop asked. You're a very wise person."

Eve smiling, biting her lip. “That doesn’t answer my question, though.”

Oliver nodded. “The answer is; I’m running toward something. Something I want very much. Only I didn’t want to come to you until I was fully committed to my decision. I’m running to you, Eve. To your life. Because I want us to be together.”

If she hadn’t felt the chill of the air on her cheeks or the very definite tingle all throughout her body, she would have sworn she was dreaming. Her heart raced, blood pounding in her ears. She was afraid she had misheard him.

She hadn’t. He held out his hands with a warm smile. Eve took a chance and laid her hands in his. They were warm, and gentle, but strong. “The moment you sang to me… I knew I’d fallen in love with you. Head over heels. I had no idea what to do. But I couldn’t forget you. I knew I had to make this choice. I can’t be without you.”

“You did this for me?” It seemed so unbelievable.

“Mostly. The rest because I feel so drawn to your community. You showed me a side of life I wasn’t aware of. I didn’t even know how dissatisfied I was with the direction my life had taken. But it was you, showing it to me, that made a difference. If it were anybody else I would have moved on without a second thought, I guess. You were what did it. I love you."

Tears filled Eve's eyes. To think, just minutes earlier she had been filled with sadness, loneliness. She had questioned her feelings, and whether or not she would ever be happy again. Now this.

"My heart is yours," she whispered, beaming with pure joy. "It's all yours, and only yours."

Epilogue

Eve stood at the kitchen sink, washing up after supper. Her father and Caleb were in the fields, along with Oliver.

She smiled when she saw them approaching. They had gone out to put the horses under cover in the barn. It looked as though there was a storm coming up over the horizon.

Had it really been a year since the storm which brought Oliver into her life? Very close to it, if not a year to the day. So much had happened in the months since that fateful night.

Such as Oliver's baptism into the faith, and their wedding.

She looked down at her hand, in the soapy water. A gold ring glinted there. It seemed so funny, seeing it. There were times when it caught her eye as she went about her day, and she would be startled. Was it possible that this was the symbol of Oliver's love and commitment?

It was.

They were living with Eve's Daed and brother until they got on their feet. Oliver was taking to the Amish way of life very well, almost as though he were born to it. It wouldn't be long until he knew enough about his trade to move the two of them into their own home. The land had already been purchased for the by the community, but Oliver needed to know a bit more about farming and managing the land before it was wise for him to take on his own farm. They would run their own farm stand—Oliver's business knowledge would come in handy, and Eve's love of gardening would help as well.

It would only be a matter of time, and Eve's heart sang when she thought of a home of her own and a family of her own.

In the meantime, she enjoyed caring for her father and Caleb. They needed a woman around the house to cook and clean for them. Once Eve left, the other women in the community would make it a point to care for them, so the job wouldn't fall completely on her shoulders while she busied herself with getting her household in order…and, of course, while they started a family.

There were still challenges from time to time, as Oliver adjusted to life with the Amish. Having been raised in a world of electronics and instant communication with the entire world, it was quite a change in thinking to be so secluded, so suddenly. And yet, he wasn't. One of the observations he made most frequently in the early days of his life in the Ordung was of feeling more connected to friends and neighbors than ever before. As it turned out, being able to push a button to speak with someone halfway around the world was nothing in comparison to simply chatting with a friend in passing. It was more satisfying, he said.

He never regretted it for a moment, though. And as Eve saw her husband walking up the steps to the house, the smile on his face reminded her of how Gott brought them together to show Oliver his true place in the world. It was clear he belonged there, with them. With her. She thanked Gott every day for the chance to take care of Oliver, then and always.

About the Author

Be the first to find out about Hannah's New Books Click Here to Find Out How

I would like to thank you for taking the time to download my book. I really hope that you enjoyed it as much as I enjoyed writing it.

If you feel able I would love for you to give the book a short review on Amazon.

If you want to keep up to date with all of my latest releases then please like my FACEBOOK PAGE

Many thanks once again, all my love.

Hannah.

LATEST BOOKS

Amish Romance Mega book
Amish Love and Romance Collection

The Amish Detective: The King Family Arsonist
The Amish Gift
Becoming Amish
The Amish Foundling Girl
The Heartbroken Amish Girl
The Missing Amish Girl
Amish Joy
The Amish Detective
Amish Double
The Burnt Amish Girl

AMISH ROMANCE SERIES

AMISH HEARTACHE

AMISH REFLECTIONS: AMISH ANTHOLOGY COLLECTION

MORE AMISH REFLECTIONS : ANOTHER AMISH ANTHOLOGY COLLECTION

THE AMISH WIDOW AND THE PREACHER'S SON

AN AMISH CHRISTMAS WITH THE BONTRAGER SISTERS

A BIG BEAUTIFUL AMISH COURTSHIP

AMISH YOUNG SPRING LOVE BOX SET

AMISH PARABLES SERIES BOX SET

AMISH HEART SHORT STORY COLLECTION

AMISH HOLDUP

AN AMISH TRILOGY BOX SET

AMISH ANGUISH

SHORT AMISH ROMANCE STORIES

AMISH BONTRAGER SISTERS 2 - THE COMPLETE SECOND SEASON

AMISH BONTRAGER SISTERS - THE COMPLETE FIRST SEASON

THE AMISH BROTHER'S BATTLE

AMISH OUTSIDER

AMISH FORGIVENESS AND FRIENDSHIP

THE AMISH OUTSIDER'S LIE

AMISH VANITY

AMISH NORTH

AMISH YOUNG SPRING LOVE SHORT STORIES SERIES

THE AMISH BISHOP'S DAUGHTER

AN AMISH ARRANGEMENT

AMISH REJECTION

AMISH BETRAYAL

THE AMISH BONTRAGER SISTERS SHORT STORIES SERIES

AMISH RETURN

AMISH BONTRAGER SISTERS COMPLETE COLLECTION

AMISH APOLOGY

AMISH UNITY

AMISH DOUBT

AMISH FAMILY

THE ENGLISCHER'S GIFT

AMISH SECRET

AMISH PAIN

THE AMISH PARABLES SERIES

THE AMISH BUILDER

THE AMISH PRODIGAL SON

AMISH PERSISTENCE

THE AMISH GOOD SAMARITAN

Made in the USA
San Bernardino, CA
29 January 2019